FLIPPING
FORWARD
TWISTING
BACKWARD

Published by
PEACHTREE PUBLISHING COMPANY INC.
1700 Chattahoochee Avenue
Atlanta, Georgia 30318-2112
PeachtreeBooks.com

Text © 2022 by Alma Fullerton
Illustrations © 2022 by Sarah Mensinga

Cover design by Kate Gartner
Interior design and typeset by Adela Pons
Edited by Catherine Frank

Printed and bound in May 2022 at Lake Book Manufacturing, Melrose Park, IL, USA

10 9 8 7 6 5 4 3 2 1
First Edition
ISBN: 978-1-68263-366-3

Cataloging-in-Publication Data is available from the Library of Congress

ALMA FULLERTON

H MENSINGA

FLIPPING

FORWARD

TWISTING

BACKWARD

Ω

PEACHTREE

ATLANTA

To Mrs. Monds and to all educators who not only understand that every child can learn but go above and beyond to find out how they learn

—A. F.

ABOUT THE TYPE

This book was designed using the font Sassoon Book. Dr. Rosemary Sassoon and Adrian Williams developed and designed the Sassoon family of typefaces specifically with and for children and especially for use in children's books. It uses easily recognizable letters that produce a well-defined word shape.

Sassoon is a registered trademark of Dr. Rosemary Sassoon and Adrian Williams. For more information about the Sassoon family of typefaces, visit SassoonFont.co.uk

FULL-DAY SUNDAY PRACTICE

In the gym club
there's always someone
who flies higher
and works harder
than everyone else.

In the gym club
there's always someone
who pushes to be
number one.

In the gym club
there's always someone
who can do
anything.

When I am
in the gym club
that someone
is me.

There's
no better feeling
than being number one
when everywhere else
you're last in line.

FIRST LINEUP

After an hour of
conditioning
Coach Tami has us
all line up.

"What do you want to
work on today?"

As she goes down the line
each of us tells her which skills
we want to work on.

When it's my turn
I say my triple-full on the track
and my giant pirouette
full twist full away
on the bars.

I've never tried a
triple-full on the track
but last week I accidentally
over-rotated on a double
so why not?

LUNCH BREAK HOMEWORK

Emma Lea Donovan.

She's been my BFF
since we were three.

We met
in Tumble for Tots.

She knows all
my secrets
and I know hers.

During our gymnastics lunch break
Emma Lea helps me
with my homework.

We sit in the corner
book opened.

Taking my pencil,
she helps me
by filling in the right words.

I say, "I wish I had smarts
like you."

Coach Tami looks up
from where she's sitting and says,
"Claire, you have plenty of smarts.
You pick up a routine
faster than anyone."

She glances as Emma Lea
finishes my work.
"And you can
trick your friend
into doing your homework.
That takes
real smarts."

Hearing Coach Tami
say I have real smarts
makes my heart soar higher
than Simone Biles
on the uneven bars.

ONE STEP AT A TIME

For every skill
I practice
I do it

one
        step

at a time.

Perfect the
giant pirouette.

Stop.

Perfect the twist
with a spotter.

Stop

and again.

Stop

and again.

You need to have
every step perfect
before you can
put it all together.
Otherwise
there's a good chance
you'll take the bar in the head.

SMARTS

No matter how hard
I try
I can't read well
or write nice
like Emma Lea.

Letters

float, blur
backward
forward
upside down

all mixed up.

SAMЯTƧ
ЯAMSⱢS
ƧARSⱯT

All I see is

a stupid jungle of letters.

THE BIGGEST CHEERLEADER

Over the music
I can always hear
one voice
above the others
cheering on everyone.

"Come on, you got it, Willow."

"Yeeeaah, Ali!"

"Awesome job, Dar."

"Woo-hoo! Claire!"

Over everything else
we can all hear
our team
cheerleader.

So when she lands
her Tsuk pike
on the vault
the first time
we all yell

"Good job, Emma Lea!"

I'm so lucky she's
my best friend.

SECOND LINEUP

At the end of practice
Coach Tami goes down the line
again.

We're supposed to tell her which skills
we've improved on.

She never asks
what we perfected
because all we
need to know
is how we
improved.

MOM

"Coach Tami said
I can pick up a routine
faster than anyone."

"Amazing," Mom says.

"I totally nailed my beam routine," I tell her.

"Fantastic. I would love to have seen it."

"She says if I keep it up
I'll get to the state championships
no problem."

Mom wraps her arms around me
and holds me tight.
"Of course you will.
You are amazing.
But right now
get upstairs to finish
your homework so you can
get past fifth grade."

"Ugh."
I still have to
write a poem
and writing
is almost as bad
as reading.

HOMEWORK

Mrs. Rose told me
to take my time.

So when I write
my poem
I take my time.

I sit in my room

slowly shaping

each letter so they all fit

between the lines.

After a billion tries
and a mountain of
crumpled paper

I do it

without eraser marks.

I carefully slide
my perfect poem
into my binder
so it doesn't get too crinkled.

I don't even have time
to switch on the TV
and Mom is yelling
bedtime.

EARLY MORNING CONDITIONING

5:30 a.m. comes fast
the morning after a full day
of practice.

The rain hitting
my window
makes me want to
curl up tighter
under my blankets.

I roll out of bed
grab a bagel
and wait for Coach Tami
to pick me up
for some one-on-one
training.

There's no sleep for
gymnasts pushing
to go all the way
to the Olympics
someday.

KNOCKED OUT BY WORDS

By 8:00 I'm sitting
right beside Emma Lea
at school.

I smooth my poem
out on my desk
and wait for Mrs. Rose to say
"Good job, Claire."

But Mrs. Rose only frowns
when she sees
my poem.

"Claire, apparently you didn't

pay attention

to our chat," she says.
"It's obvious you didn't

understand

when I told you to
take your time."

Her words
knock the wind out of me
faster than missing the bar
and landing flat on your stomach.

Before tears
well up in my eyes
that defeated feeling
flips into anger
and sails across the room
on my crumpled-up
poem.

MISS UNDERSTOOD

When my paper hits Melanie Watson
I don't say sorry
even though
I am.

Instead I stand
and yell, "I am all about
understanding,
Mrs. Rose!
I totally understood you.
I am Miss Understood."

Mrs. Rose's eyes scrunch
until they are such little slits.

I doubt she can see me
copycatting her.

But when the class laughs
her eyes pop open
as wide as jumbo marbles.

"Well, Miss Understood, you
can march yourself over to see
the vice principal right now."

FIRST-NAME BASIS

The office people and I
have been old friends
since I was in kindergarten.

"Good morning, Judith," I say.
"I'm here to chat with Mr. McKay."

Judith rolls her eyes
and presses her button.

"Mr. McKay, Claire is here
to see you."

There are twelve Claires
in our school.

But he knows
it's me.

MR. McKAY

"What brings you here today, Claire?"

Mr. McKay
Edward, Eddie, Ed
Mr. Ed looks bored
when I step into his office.

I grab a piece of pizza
from the box they keep there
for hungry kids.

And I am hungry.
5:30 breakfast
was hours ago.

I'm in early enough today that
the pizza is still hot.

The chair whooshes
when I plunk myself
into it.

My butt fits perfectly into
the memory foam.

"It's Mrs. Rose, Mr. McKay.
She's picking on me again
and making me angry."

"Is that so?"

"Yes, she's saying I didn't
take my time writing my poem
when I did."

"You were sent here
because of that?" Mr. McKay asks.

"I worked really hard
at making it all neat and tidy.
She said I didn't understand our talk.
But I understood everything.
She's the one who doesn't
understand
so I crumpled up the poem
and threw it at Melanie Watson.

BY ACCIDENT.

It was with this hand
—the right or is this left?" I ask.

"Right," he says.

"Right. I'm not so good at aiming
with this hand."

"So then she sent you to the office?" he asks.

"Yes, well, no. Not exactly then . . ."
And I explain what happened.
"Now you see.
I didn't do anything."

"I understand she made you mad
but I think you need
to apologize to Mrs. Rose
when you get back to class

for being disrespectful."

I wiggle in the seat
because I don't
want to apologize
to someone who started it
but I know I should anyway.

"Yes, sir."

TRYING TO READ

When I get back to class
everyone is silent reading.
I whisper-apologize
to Mrs. Rose.
Then sit
and pull out my book.

My letters are
flipping forward
twisting backward
just like a giant pirouette
        full twist
                full away
on the uneven bars.

If I could flip as smoothly
as my letters
I could easily perfect
that move
and make it
all the way to the state championships
with a perfect score.

RECESS

Even though
we aren't supposed
to share snacks
Emma Lea offers me
half of her cream-filled cake.

"Thanks.
I'm kind of full
from office pizza
but there's always
room for cake," I say.

"There's pizza in the office?"
Emma Lea asks. I don't bother answering her.
"How was morning practice?" she asks.

"Grueling.
An hour of conditioning
and half an hour of running
my floor routine
over and over."

"Do you have it?"

"Yep."

I'd show her but ever since
I landed on my face
attempting a front tuck
when I was seven
gymnastics is banned
from the playground.

DAD AND ME TIME

Mom and Dad
got a divorce two years ago
when Dad decided
he was done judging people
in the courtroom
and decided to buy a hobby farm.

Mom wanted nothing to do with that.

She calls the farm his
midlife crisis
and thinks he must have had
another crisis when he married June
last year
only four months
after he met her.

Of course June loves
the farming life.

Bethany and I love spending
the summer at the farm too
and June is okay
but she's no Mom.

During the school year
we don't get to see Dad
so every Monday
after school
is supposed to be
Dad and me time.

Not that we
can do anything but chat
because he's halfway
across the country.

MONDAY AFTER SCHOOL

When Dad pops
onto the screen
he's bottle-feeding a black lamb
with my baby brother, Jeremy,
hanging out of a knapsack
on his back.

Jeremy is pulling on
Dad's man-bun.

Dad's got goatee stubble.

"Are you trying to grow
a beard to blend in
with your goats?" I ask.

"You like it?"
He strokes his chin.
"I've always wanted
to grow one."

"It looks very hipster."

"Not sure if that's a compliment
or not but I'll take it."
Dad laughs.

A white lamb nudges
the black one away
from the bottle.
"Not your turn, little fella," Dad says,
pulling the bottle away.

"You look busy."

"Not too busy
to talk to you."
Dad is smiling
but he's looking at
something behind the screen.

"Summer," he calls.
"Grab the other bottle
and feed the white lamb."

"Can't. I'm helping Mama."

June's six-year-old daughter
pokes her head
around the screen
and into the camera frame.
"Hi, Claire!"

"Hey, Summer."

She races away,
laughing.

"She's gotten bigger," I say.
"How's June?"

"She's good.
She's—"

The unfed white lamb
springs up and bumps the table
and everything
goes blank.

Call ended.

I wait a few minutes
but I don't expect him to
come back.

He's too busy with
his new and improved
fun farming family
to spend time with us
anymore.

BETHANY

I head up to Bethany's room.

"How was the call
with Dad?"

"Same old
    same old," I say.

"Too busy to talk?"
she asks.

"Yep," I say.

She nods and sighs
because she totally gets it.
I sit on the bed beside her.

"I miss the old Dad.
The one who had time
for us," I say.

"Me too."

Our sad sneaks into the room
and settles down in the empty space
between us
just like Dad's old cat, Sugar, used to
before Mom told Dad to take her
with him when he left.

FAKING

After a few minutes
Bethany turns into her
usual Miss Bossy Boo self.

"Claire, stop jumping."
"Claire, read your book."
"Claire, you know
Mom will drill you."

Bethany is so bossy
she should be a teacher
when she grows up.

I flip off the bed,
knocking her ceiling light.

We don't breathe
until it stops shaking.

"READ."
She bosses again.

"You're not reading."

"I can text
and read at the same time."

She stretches the "I"
like an over-split.

I flop on my stomach
and watch the letters
do cartwheels.

I turn my pages
when Bethany does.

We're like two of a kind.
Or rather
I try to be
just like her.

Except she's reading (mostly)
and I can't.

HOW I KNOW

Mom comes home
from her shift at the hospital
exhausted.

I bring her a plate
of spaghetti.

"Thanks, kiddo," she says.
"How's your dad?"

"Fine," I say.
"He has a man-bun
and he's growing a beard now."

Mom chuckles.
She picks up the book I was
fake reading.
"This looks interesting.
What is it about?"

"I finished it today.
It's about a girl who steals a dog
but in the end she returns it."

"Sounds like a good book."

"It was."

Mom is easy to trick
when she asks about
what I'm reading.
I always pick books

I can find in audio
on the library site.

I may not be able to read
what the words say
but my memory
is awesome.

MOTHER-DAUGHTER TIME

Dad may slough off
our time together
a lot
but Mom
never does.

Even though she's a surgeon
she makes time
for just us.

We sit on the couch
snuggled into each other
watching our favorite
talent show.

She doesn't ask once
if I have any homework.

This is our time
and not even that
can interrupt it.

MORNING JOG

Bethany always takes
Emma Lea and me
jogging with her
on Tuesday mornings.

She says it's because
she likes to spend time
with us
but I think it's because
Tuesday is the only day
her boyfriend can't go
with her.

Next year
when she gets her driver's license
we'll go to the track
at the fitness center
but for now we just go
five times around the block.

Even with all of our training
Bethany could easily
out-lap me and Emma Lea
twice
but she doesn't.
She slows her normal pace
to stay by us
and listen to
all of our
fifth-grade
gossip.

For a Bossy Boo,
Bethany can be
a pretty awesome
sister.

LOVE LETTER

A fake love letter
from Eva to Jake
finds its way
into the hands of
Mrs. Rose.

A love letter
not written by the girl
whose name is at the bottom.
It makes Eva cry so hard
she's gulping air
and snorting snot.

"I AM LIVID."
Mrs. Rose raises
her voice.
"There is
no lunch recess
until I find out
who wrote that note."

Her words make
Eva even more
upset.

Tony's sneer
and lack of protest
screams that he wrote it.
But there's no fessing up
when it comes to Tony

and I'm not a tattletale.

I raise my hand.
"Mrs. Rose, I did it."

CALLED OUT

I stare at Eva,
sending an *I really didn't* message
when I say, "Sorry."

But the only one getting
my message is Mrs. Rose.

"Claire, you didn't write this note."

"No way she could have," Tony says.
"The words are spelled properly
and the letters are all facing
the right direction and she's
SPED."

Anger bubbles up
from my feet all the way
to my head like
an out-of-control tumbler
who's about to crash
right into their spotter.

"I'm not special ed!"
I smash my desk
into the back of his chair.

"Claire!" Mrs. Rose gives me her
exasperated look
so I stand and stomp myself
to the office.

The fact that Tony knew
what was in the letter
makes me know for sure
he wrote it.

LIAR LIAR

Mrs. Rose is always
calling me a
    liar.

If it's not about writing a letter
it's about not taking my time.

Okay, this time
maybe I did lie.

I didn't write the letter
but it wasn't fair
that everyone was getting in trouble
because of one person.

And Mrs. Rose didn't have to
get mad at me
like *that*
when it was Tony
who was way
out of line.

That was just
rude.

NO TIME

"Mr. McKay is at an all-day meeting.
He's not here today.
Miss Wright is filling in for him,"
Judith says.

"I need to talk to him.
He always mashes
Mrs. Rose's baked-potato
words."

"What?" she asks.

"He makes me feel better," I explain,
peeking through the blinds
and sure enough
it is Miss Wright
sitting at Mr. McKay's desk.

She's no good at
mashing potatoes
so I have to stick
with a hard
baked-potato
insult.

NOTE TO SELF

Having an anti-slam thingamabob
on the top of an office door
makes an office person
bite her lip to keep from laughing
when you attempt to slam the door
and it closes super slow
even though you yank
your very hardest.

KIND WORDS

When I get back
to class, Mrs. Rose
does a pretty good job
of mashing her own
baked-potato words.

"Class, now that Claire is back
I want to explain why
I don't think she wrote the note,"
Mrs. Rose says.
"Although Claire can
cause a stir at times
she has a very kind heart.
I simply knew that she would
not have harassed other students
in that way, and
that letter is harassment.
And WRONG
very, very wrong.

Calling each other names
is not acceptable
in this class.
We are a community.
I don't want to hear of any more
name-calling."

I do have a kind heart
and would never have written

that note

even if I could have.

But I didn't expect to hear
kind words about me
come from Mrs. Rose's mouth.

SILENT READING

THICK

                                               WALLS

                    SURROUND

MY

                    WORDS

                                  SO

        THEY

                                                    CAN

    NEVER

CONNECT

SILENT READING

THICK

                                                  WALLS

                   SURROUND

MY

                   WORDS

                                    SO

        THEY

                                                          CAN

NEVER

CONNECT

AFTER SCHOOL

On the bus
Eva sits in the seat
right beside
me and Emma Lea.

"I know you didn't write
that letter," she whispers.
"I knew right away
you wouldn't.
You were only confessing
so we could go to recess."

"It wasn't fair
everyone, even you,
had to stay behind," I say.
"You were the one being bullied."

"Right?" Eva says.

"That was like
double punishment,"
Emma Lea says.

"It sure was."

The bus comes to
Emma Lea's stop
and she gets up.
"See you in a bit, Claire."

"Yup, less than an hour."
She high-fives me and
heads down the aisle.

Eva looks like she thinks
we're having a party
and didn't invite her.

"Gymnastics.
Tuesday night
Thursday night
Saturday morning
and all-day Sunday."

"Oh.
That's a lot of training."

"Yup. And I go for an
extra two hours
Monday morning."

"Wow. You must be really dedicated."

"Oh yeah."

She smiles again
and I'm relieved
that she knows there's
no party.

Eva has already had a bad day.
And thinking you're not invited to a party
on a day like that is worse than
throwing up all over the mat
during a state competition.

WARM-UPS

Today Coach Tami has me lead
warm-ups and conditioning
for three reasons.

One: She knows
I'm not going to let
anyone fool around.

Two: I can use the same
warm-ups she does
with me Monday
mornings.

Three: Today Mom
is here watching
and that's a rare thing.

Although Mom loves to see
when I land things right,
being a surgeon, and a mom,
she overthinks accidents
that could happen.

Some days she's fine
but some days
her nerves are shot
and she can't handle it
when I fall flat
on my face
and that happens
a lot.

MOM AND ME

During break

I curl up next to Mom
in the parents' gallery
and breathe in
her soapy smell.

"You're doing well."
She wraps her arms
around me.

"Almost have the full twist
full away," I say.
"But I'm messing up a lot
and that last fall really hurt."

Mom takes in a deep breath
and lets it out.
"Are you okay?"

"I am now."

"You'll get it," she says.
I believe she believes I will
but she wraps me up tighter
in her arms like she's trying
to stop me from falling again.

A BAD JOKE

At school Melanie takes a
HUGE bite
of her sandwich
and pulls out a couple of worms.

She screams.

The thunk of her head
hitting the desk
causes the lunch monitors
to freeze with their mouths
hanging open.

Tony laughs
so loud he's snorting.

I'm scared
because Melanie is
out like a light
but I also can't keep from laughing.

The rest of the class
is laughing or giggling too.

By the time
Mr. McKay arrives
Melanie is conscious.

He helps her
out of her seat and
walks with her toward
the classroom door.

Jodi Turner is hot on their tails,
talking a mile a minute.

"There were worms
WORMS
and she ate half of one!"

Melanie moans
grabs her stomach
and pukes on the floor.

ACCUSED

I STILL
canNOT
stop giggling
even though
I don't think
it's one bit funny.

Mrs. Rose says,

"Claire . . . ?

Please tell me
you did not put the worms
in Melanie's sandwich
as a joke."

What happened to the
Claire has a kind heart thing?

The laughter
flips out of me
and I shake my head no
real quick.

"I BET she did!" Jodi shouts.
"She laughed the whole time."

I want to scream
So did Tony
and most of the other kids
but instead I only sit
QUIET
like I've lost my voice
and can't deny
Jodi's accusation.
Now everyone
is going to blame me.

NOT GUILTY

"Innocent until proven guilty"
That's what Mr. McKay always tells everyone.
But Mrs. Rose thinks
I might have done it
and watches me
like a dog
watches you eat
popcorn.

That woman has a
circle of eyes
around her head
and she sees everything
except who really
put the worms
in Melanie's sandwich.

TIA AND TRISH

Emma Lea comes over
and when we get home
we have to entertain my twin cousins
Tia and Trish
while Mom and Aunt Tracey plan
a family dinner.

Watching Tia and Trish is a
piece of cake
because they love Emma Lea and think
I'm a super-cousin.

Like most times
we do gymnastics with them
in the yard.
But then they want
me to read to them.

Emma Lea says,
"I'll read it for you."

But Trish takes the book
from her.
"We want Claire.
She does cool voices and stuff."

FAKING IT

The letters are
tumbling across the page
in their own floor routine.

There's a bear
and a rabbit on the cover
so I use the pictures
to make up a story to go with it.

After the first few pages
Tia and Trish giggle.

"You're reading all the
wrong words,"
Tia says.

I swallow back my frustration
because I can't cry
in front of my little cousins.

"Get Emma Lea to read,
because I think it's
a stupid baby book."

Tia and Trish put on
sulky faces and tears pool
in their eyes.

I look away because
I just handed my sad
to my little cousins.

"I was joking.
It's an awesome book!" I say.
"Your mom told me
you two were reading
and I want to hear
you read."

I hand them the book
and take back my sad
so they don't feel it
anymore.

EASY

If reading is so easy
that five-year-olds can do it

why can't I?

TRICKING MRS. ROSE

I stare at the words
on the page for so long
it makes me want to
throw up.

So before Mrs. Rose
calls me to reading group
I say, "Bet you can't read this, David."

"Can too,
I can read anything."

I show him the section
I'm having trouble
reading.

"That's simple
'Hurry up, Becca. Run!
The supermarket will be closing soon
and we need groceries for tomorrow's party.'"

"Good job. You're right," I say.

"Claire!" Mrs. Rose shouts.

"What?"

She gives me her
you know what look.

"I didn't do anything."

"You were cheating.
Claire, if you ever want to graduate
you're going to have to
stop fooling around
and try to do your own work."

Mrs. Rose's words
slither through the silence
like a snake sneaking up
on its prey.
They wrap around me
so tight it feels like
I'm being choked.

Crying in front of everyone
would only make
things worse
so to fight the tears
I glare at Mrs. Rose
and yell:

"Maybe you should just
 shut up!"

Mrs. Rose's face is pinched
like a dried apple
and she's shaking mad.

"I'm going to the office now," I say.

THE LONG WALK

Today it's a long walk
to the office
because this time
I know I really did
something wrong.

Telling a teacher
to shut up
is bad.

I try so hard.

By the time I get to the office
I am crying
for real.

REAL TROUBLE

"What's going on today, Claire?" Mr. McKay asks.

"I told Mrs. Rose to shut up," I say,
wiping a tear from my cheek.

I take a big sniff
and Mr. McKay hands me a Kleenex.

"But she said I was fooling around
and that I'd never
graduate.
          GRAD . . . U . . . ATE!

I'm in FIFTH GRADE for Pete's sake.
Who is Pete anyway?"

"Pete?" Mr. McKay looks confused.

"The Pete's sake guy?"

He shrugs.

"Anyhow, that's when
I told her to shut up," I say.
"So I wouldn't cry in front of everyone."

"Ah. Do you think it's a good idea
to tell a teacher to shut up?"

"No,
but I wasn't fooling around.
And it's totally not my fault."

I LIKE BOOKS BUT . . .

"It all started with that stupid Becca running
in the book.
I think Becca needs to run
far away from Mrs. Rose
and her dumb
'work on sounding out the

   *A E I O U*s
   and sometimes *Y*s.'"

"You don't like reading, Claire?"

"It's not that I don't like books.
I do. Especially when
someone reads to me.

It's that I don't understand
how anyone expects a person to put
words together
to make a sentence when it takes
so long
to figure out the
mess of letters
in one word
that you forget what the words
before it were."

Mr. McKay tilts his head
and looks at me for
long enough I think
I said WAY too much.

WHEN I READ

"What happens to the letters
when you read?" Mr. McKay asks.

"It's like they are having
a dance party on the page
without me. It makes me
dizzier than a kid
spinning in circles."

"Hmm . . ."
He presses a button
on his phone.
"Judith, can you get me
Claire's standardized test results?"

"She won't find them," I say.
"My parents opted us out.
They don't believe in them.
Why would you need the scores
anyway?"

"I wanted to see if we missed something."

"Something bad?" I ask.

"Nothing Mrs. French
couldn't help you with."

"The Mrs. French who works
with kids with
learning disabilities?"

"Yes, that Mrs. French."

"You think maybe
I have a learning disability too?"

"Maybe," he says.

Maybe he's right.

MIXED EMOTIONS

I don't know
if I should feel
    scared
            or relieved.

What if I go
see Mrs. French
and everyone
            just
                finds
                    out

I am stupid.

DURING RECESS

Everyone is still talking
about the worm incident.

Melanie confronts me
when I step outside.
"I know you put those worms
in my sandwich, Claire."

"I didn't."
I look around for backup
but Emma Lea left
for a dentist appointment
and I can't see Eva
anywhere.

"I didn't do it
and I'm sorry you got sick."

"Yeah, right," Jodi says.
"You're stupid if you think
we believe you."

"She's stupid anyway."
Melanie gets right up
in my face.
"Even Mrs. Rose says so."

"I'm not stupid.
And she did NOT say that."
Mrs. Rose didn't call me stupid.
I'm sure of it.
"Fooling around"
doesn't mean stupid.

I'm not just stupid.
I'm not.
I can't be.

SURROUNDED

"Yeah, you are STUPID."
Tony comes from out of nowhere
and butts his stupid head
into our private conversation.

"AM NOT!"

"Are too," Tony says.

The three of them crowd me
and I feel trapped
on the playground.

"Get away from me!"

"No." He pushes me toward Melanie.
"YOU will never even graduate."

"Yeah, Claire."
She pushes me back to Tony.
I am being passed
around like a hot potato.

Tony shoves me
and I fall.
"Did you all see that?
Stupid Claire just tripped
on her own feet."

I can't stop the tears
from flowing.

A group of kids
surrounds us
but there is
no backup for me.

Sand fills my eyes,
mixing with tears.
It drips down my face
in sparkly blobs.

I hear someone run off
but I don't see who.

"You want to see stupid?"
I scream.

I jump to my feet
and ram into Tony
with all my might.

He falls over a boingy horse
for kindergarteners,
causing it to KICK back.

His whole shirt is
soaked in blood.
I can't believe what
I just did.

Everyone backs away,
making a space for me
to get through
so I take off.

YOU WILL NEVER BE

I collapse on the grass
by a tree in the back
of the schoolyard.

I can't catch my breath.
It feels like I flipped off
the uneven bars and landed
flat on my back
except there were no bars
and no floor
and no mat.

Only ONE big
imaginary fall.

All I hear is
"You're stupid.
You're trouble.
You'll never be anything."

A caterpillar crawls
across the grass.

Slow and innocent
munching its way
to becoming
a butterfly.

When I will stay
nothing.

My insides explode
red and fiery.

I raise my fist
and smash it down
on that caterpillar

HARD!

"YOU WILL NEVER BE
A BUTTERFLY!"

NO LABELS

Mom is

not impressed

because knocking out a kid's teeth
brings one of your parents
to the office.

With Dad so far away
Mom is the one.

I'm not really listening
while she begs Mr. McKay
not to expel me.

I half-listen
as Mr. McKay agrees.
I'll only be suspended
for the rest of today and tomorrow
because someone
spoke up for me.

They said

Melanie, Jodi, and Tony
bullied me first, so
Tony's missing teeth
aren't my fault. Kind of.

I tune in, sort of,
when I hear Mom ask,
"What about the three children
who were teasing Claire?"

"They will be dealt with."

LEARNING DISABILITIES

I'm all ears when Mr. McKay says,
"While you're here, Dr. Cardin,
I wanted to share that
I think it might be
a good idea
to have Claire
tested for

   learning disabilities.

She's having
trouble reading and writing.

These tests will give us an idea
of how to help her
learn to read better."

But Mom says,
"Claire doesn't need a special test.
She reads just fine.
If she can't read
how did she get to fifth grade?"

"We didn't know.
Claire excels in other areas.
She has developed strategies
to learn in other ways.
Like listening carefully and remembering.
The fact that she was opted out
of standardized testing made it
a little harder to catch.

But even with the test
children like Claire
can slip by."

Mom sighs.
"I'm sure if Claire
spent more time doing her homework
we wouldn't have this problem.
I think maybe
she's training too much.
Maybe she's too tired to learn.
She doesn't have
a learning disability."

Please, Mr. McKay.
Please tell her
that's not it.

"It could be."

My brain is
cracked like
the tile under Mr. McKay's desk.

"You don't want to test her
just to make sure?" Mr. McKay asks.

"I don't want my child labeled.
She doesn't need
other children thinking
she's stupid."

"Too late for that," I say.

SOME NERVE

Mom grips
the steering wheel
so tight I can see
indents in the
leather cover.
"That man has
some nerve
telling me there's
something wrong
with your head.

You come from a
long line of
highly educated
very smart people.

I teach things to my children.
We read all the time.
I'm not a
bad mother.
There is no way a child of
mine has a learning disability."

Staring straight ahead
she takes a deep breath.

"No child of mine
has limited possibilities.

You spend twenty hours a week
in the gym. Maybe cutting back
will give you more time
and more focus
to learn."

I nod.

But everything outside

the window blurs through
lopsided tears.

POSSIBILITIES

I always thought
my possibilities
were endless.

My dream is to go
to the Olympics
but I'm not
delusional.

I know no matter
how hard I work
it might not
happen.

Then what?

Can I be a doctor
or lawyer or
whatever
I want to be
with a learning
disability?

Is that what Mom
is afraid of?

Maybe I haven't thought
hard enough about
what having a learning disability

would mean
for my future.

BUT IF

If I don't have a learning disability
that means I am

     just

           plain

                 stupid.

WORDS I KNOW

I can read
dog
because God
doesn't have perky ears
and a droopy tail

(at least I don't think so).

DOORS THAT SLAM

Mom says,
"Can you go read
in your room?
I need to call your father."

"No, thank you."

"I beg your pardon?"
Mom spins around
fast to look at me.

"I don't want to read."

"It wasn't a request.
The more you read
the better you'll get."

"But you asked."

"Claire, I've had enough
of you today.
Just GO READ
or I'm not taking you
to practice tonight."

"It's Emma Lea's mom's turn to drive anyway."

There is no
anti-slam thingamabob
on my bedroom door.

It slams just fine.

IN MY ROOM

I cover my head
with my pillow
so I can't hear
Mom screaming
at Dad
about me
over the phone
anymore.

I curl into a tight ball.
I am not stupid.
I am not.

Mrs. French will figure out
how to help me.
She has to help.
If she doesn't
it will mean everyone
is right.

BFF SUPPORT

In the car, I tell Emma Lea
about the afternoon she missed at school
while she was at the dentist.

"I wish I'd been there to help," she says.

"Mom says I train too much
and I'm too tired for learning."

"OMG, is she going to
take you out of
gymnastics?"

"She might as well.
She told Coach Tami
no more extra practices."

Emma Lea hugs me
as much as possible anyway
while we're both in seat belts.

"Emma Lea, what if I'm just stupid?"

"You one hundred percent
are NOT stupid.
Besides, Josh sees Mrs. French.
No one calls him stupid."

"Tony does," I tell her.

Words hurt.

"Tony's a jerk.
He doesn't count.
You'll prove them WRONG,"
Emma Lea whispers.
"You're going to become
a world-class gymnast."

Sometimes words
can be great too.

AWESOMENESS

Tired, unfocused gymnasts

can't tuck mount
turn
       back handspring
              step
                     layout
TURN
          back handspring
       back handspring
tuck dismount
off a balance beam.

       Awesome.

A thumbs-up
from my best friend
makes me feel like
I can do anything.

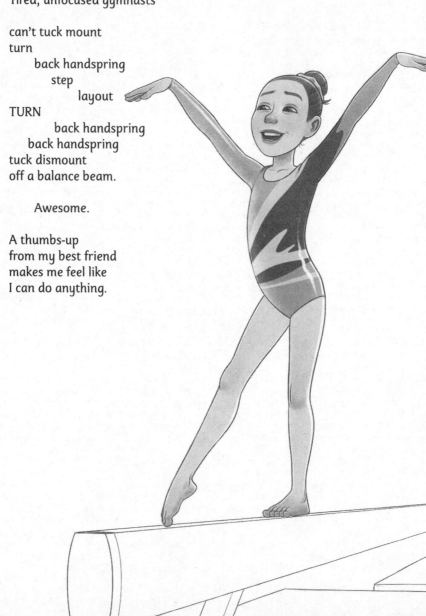

GROUNDED FROM SUNDAY PRACTICE

No all-day practice
on Sunday
is weirder than
a speechless Bethany.

I decide if I can't go to practice
I can still do conditioning.

Head and wrist rolls

Over-splits—HOLD

High toes around the room
Sixteen counts

Pike
    Squat
Pike
    Squat

Toe rise
    Toe rise
Toe rise
    Toe rise

Tuck jump
    Straight jump

Five
    reps
        each

Roll back-to-back crunches

Fifty V-snaps

Once the warm-up
and conditioning are over
I head outside to work
on my trampoline
for the rest of the
afternoon.

SENDING MYSELF TO THE OFFICE

Monday
Mrs. Rose greets me,
Tony, and Melanie

with a fake smile

the kind people give you
when they aren't
happy to see you.

I fake-smile her back
and I walk right to my desk
without saying a word
to anyone.

Mrs. Rose watches closely
as I do my work.
She stands right over me
as I write.

My printing is sloppy
and I pretend not to hear
when she *Hmmm*s me.

She sighs and says,
"Pull out your books for
silent reading."

I accidentally/on purpose
flick my eraser at
Toothless Tony.

"Hey!" Toothless says.

I stand to walk out.

"Where are you
going, Claire?"
Mrs. Rose asks.

"I flicked my eraser at Tony.
I'm going to the office."

I step into the hall,
leaving Mrs. Rose
silent.

OFFICE HELP

I grab a slice of office pizza
even though I didn't
wake up early for practice.

"I'm here because
my eraser hit Tony's head," I say.

"Mrs. Rose sent you here
for that?" Mr. McKay asks.

"No," I say.
"I sent myself.
I wanted to see you
about my reading."

"You don't have to do
something wrong
to see me about that."

"Tony's a pain.
I didn't mind."

Mr. McKay smiles.
"So, what about your reading?"

"I want to take those tests."

"You can't. Not without your
mother's permission."

"What about my dad's permission?" I ask.
"Mom thinks me having a learning disability
makes her a bad mom.
Dad probably already thinks Mom
is a bad mom because she wouldn't
raise chickens and goats with him."

"Your mother is your primary guardian
so you need her permission.
But it's not a bad idea to get
both parents' permission.
And for the record
having a child with a learning disability
doesn't make her a bad mom."

"She thinks it does.
She said
we come from a
LONG line
of very smart people," I say.
"She also said it could limit
my possibilities."

"Some very smart people
very accomplished people
have learning disabilities," he says.
"Einstein had a learning disability."

"The scientist guy
with the crazy hair?"

"Yes."

CARDS

He pulls a pile of index cards
from his desk.

"I mentioned your reading troubles
to Mrs. French
and she gave me these for you.
She said they'll help you understand
which direction your letters
are supposed to face."

"Um . . . thanks."
How did they even know
I'd be in the office today?

I take the cards.
String letters are glued
to the face of each card
in bright yellow, orange,
and blue.

As I flip through them
they look the way
all alphabet cards look.
I know it's a little *b*
because it's with a big *B.*

"I don't know how
these cards will help.
I know the alphabet.

Big letter
little letter."

Mr. McKay smiles.
"Go see Mrs. French
on your way back to class.
She'll show you how to use them."

FEELING IS BELIEVING

"Run your finger over the string
letter like this."
Mrs. French moves
her finger along the letter.
"You'll feel what
your brain inverts."

I try the *Bb*
and even though
my brain is telling me
the little letter goes like this

d

I feel it like this

b

Who knew I was seeing
it all wrong
the whole time?

"You're going to help me
without Mom's permission?" I ask.

"I'll do what I can
until you can get your mom
to agree to let us do more."

NO GOING BACK

Telling Mr. McKay
and Mrs. French
I can't read
was like doing
my very first fly
in gymnastics
all over again.

Now that I've
let go
of that bar
there's no
turning back.

All I can do is
work really hard to
stick the landing.

NOT READING WITH BETHANY

Enlisting help
to get Mom to agree
I need those tests
will make it easier
than doing it
on my own.

So instead of my usual
pretending to read
I pull out my letter cards.

"What are those?"
Bethany asks.

"Cards.
To help me learn to read.
Ed—Mr. McKay—gave them to me.
Mrs. French made them.
Don't tell Mom."

Bethany stares at me
until I lean over
and close her mouth
with my hand.

"But . . . you . . . can . . . read."

"No . . . I . . . can't.

I faked it.
I faked you out.
I faked everyone out.
I can't fake anymore.
Mr. McKay and Mrs. French know."

ONE LETTER AT A TIME

Running my finger
over the string letters
makes me imagine
which direction
they really face.

When I open my eyes
I can pick out all the *B*s
in the *Rabbit & Bear* book.

"You know how a small letter *B*
has a belly?"

"What?"

"The ball is in front of the *b*
not on the back like a . . . butt?
I don't always see it that way."

"You're not joking around?"
Bethany asks.

"Nope," I say to her.

"*B* for *belly*," she says.
"*D* for *diaper*—the butt part.
That's how you could remember.
But if you don't always see it
that way, remembering it won't help."

"Nope," I agree.
"And when teachers say
'write the way you see it'
it doesn't work well either
because I still might get it wrong."

ASKING FOR HELP

"Does Mom know?
That you can't read?" Bethany asks.

"I tried to tell her
but she won't believe me.
She won't even let me
take the tests to see
if I have a learning disability."

"Figures.
What about Dad?
Did you talk to him today?
Did you tell him?"

"He was too busy
to talk today.
Can you help me
convince Mom?"

"I can try."

Bethany and I sit
side by side
going through every letter
even the ones that don't move
when I try to focus on them.

JOGGING MY MEMORY

During our Tuesday morning jog

Emma Lea says,
"I've been Googling
and I read that sometimes
kids learn better
if they're moving.
Maybe that's you."

"I'll try anything."

"Okay, let's do
spelling words," she says.

"Great idea."
Bethany slows her jog some.
"What's the first word?"

Emma Lea answers.
"*Demolish*

    D
     E
      M
       O
        L
         I
          S
           H

Demolish
    Demolish!"

Emma Lea takes a step
with every letter
she chants.

Bethany and I join in
and we spell the word
three more times before
moving on to
the next word.

I don't know if this
will help me remember
how to spell my words
but it sure makes
learning fun.

TERRIBLE TONY

During recess
Emma Lea and I
eat our snack
then she helps me practice
keeping my letters straight.

False-teeth Tony wanders by and snorts.

"Claire is SPED!"

Emma Lea spins
to face him.
"Shut up, you jerk!"

"Make me."

Emma Lea sprays her drink box at him
and he backs away,
tripping over my outstretched leg.

"Emma Lea and Claire!"
the recess monitor shouts.
"I'm writing you up."

"He started it!" we say together.

THE ULTIMATE THREAT

Mom is being
unreasonable.

She doesn't understand.

She won't LISTEN.

She's only talking.

"If you keep this behavior up, Claire,
if you get sent to the office
or if your grades don't improve
OR if I hear any more false claims
about not being able to read

ONE MORE TIME

I will not
and I mean it, Claire,

WILL NOT
let you attend your last qualifier
for States."

MY LIFE BITES

Mom's heart-racing
    stomach-flipping
                lip-trembling
    nerve-jumping

  WORDS
        make me want to

curl up and cry

    in the corner
        she's trapped me in.

I HAVE TO DO MORE

I need more
than cards and chanting spelling words.
I need real teacher help.
So on the way to class
I duck into the learning center.

Mrs. French is sitting
at the back of the room
behind her desk.
She looks up.
"Hello, Claire."

"Hi, Mrs. French."

There are four tables
set up around the room
for working at in groups
and three beanbag chairs
in a reading corner
where a couple of kids
could take a nap.

"Are the cards helping?"

"Yes. Can I, ummm . . .
can I hang out here
sometimes?"

There are some days
I'd love to take a nap.

"I might be able to set
something up
with Mrs. Rose."
She smiles at me.

Not like a fake kind of smile
that adults have when they think
you're pathetic or something
but a real genuine smile.

"That would be great.
Thanks."

FAILING AT EVERYTHING

I miss my landing
on the vault
mess up
my beam routine
and trip
on the floor.

My only hope
is the uneven bars
but I keep having a

giant
        pirouette
                    full
                    twist
        FAIL!

AGAIN.

Giant
        pirouette
                    full
fail

SLAM.

I HAVE TO GET THIS.

Giant
        pirouette
                    full
failing FALL!

I **HAVE** TO GET THIS.

THE LEARNING CENTER

"Hello, girls," Mrs. French
greets us when we walk in.
"What can I do for you?"

"Mrs. Rose said
we could come here.
The rest of the class
is out for recess.

I know you're not supposed
to help me, so Emma Lea is."

"I can help you.
Just not officially," Mrs. French says.

She shows us some
reading games
we can play
together.

"I have something else
for you, Claire."
She hands me a stack of
different-colored
clear bookmarks.
"When you're reading
lay one of these over the words.
They'll help the letters
stop moving on you.
You'll have to find
which color works best
for you."

Maybe with help
I'll get this
reading thing
after all.

READING AT PRACTICE

When I tumble
across the floor

Emma Lea is at the end
holding up a piece of paper
with a word written on it.

I freeze
in front of her
and look around.
Others are staring.
I can feel the heat rising
to my face.

"What are you doing?"

"Read the word," she says.

"Not here."
"Why not?" she asks.

"I don't want them
to know."

"Having a learning disability
is nothing to be ashamed of," she whispers.
"No one here is going to laugh.
Besides, you want to go
to States, right?"

Once we explain
I realize there was
nothing to worry about.

The whole team
helps me
because they all
want to see me
at States.

BACK HOME

Mom is out at
Tia and Trish's karate match
with Aunt Tracey
and I have to go pee.

But there are words
printed on a sticky note
stuck to our bathroom door.

And Bethany won't
unlock the door
until I read
    those words.

"Bethany, please!"
I cross my legs.

"Sound the letters
    out loud
so you hear the words
and remember them,"
Bethany reminds me.

The letters are dancing
on the paper almost as much as
I'm dancing in the hall.

But she's not budging.

So I grab my clear yellow bookmark
and place it over the words.
I focus really hard
and stop bouncing
and the letters don't move
so much that I can't make out
the first two.

"O-b—"

"It's not a *B*," Bethany says.

I think about my string letters.

Which way is right?

"O-p-e-n

O-pen

OPEN!

The . . ." (I knew that one.)

"d—"

or is it a *b*? Or a *p*?

"No! It's a . . . b!

b-a-t-h-r-o-o-w

ba-th-roow?

No!

bathroom!

door!

Open the bathroom door!"

Bethany opens the door
and holds up her hand
but I don't have time
for high fives.

OMG

Sticky note sentences
all over the house?

Reading at practice?

Bethany and Emma Lea
are both completely
BONKERS!

Asking them to help me
so I can go to Qualifiers
was a huge mistake.

SUNDAY PRACTICE

Today
is all
about
gymnastics.

No words
to learn
no sentences
to read.

Just me and training
and I can
forget
everything
else.

TWO DAYS CAN MAKE ALL THE DIFFERENCE

Giant
    pirouette
          full twisting
    fail.

AGAIN.

Giant
    pirouette
          full twisting
    fail.

I will not give up.

NO matter how
many times

    I fail.

MORE TROUBLE

When Emma Lea
drops me off after practice
Aunt Tracey's car
is in the driveway.

Tia and Trish found one of Bethany's Post-its
on my writing notebook.

"'Mrs. Rose is an old hag.'"
Tia reads it
and then holds the paper out to Aunt Tracey.

Bethany and I freeze.

"Yeah," Trish says.
"She's a real old hag."

"Yep, the worstest old hag ever."
Tia giggles.

"OLD HAG!"

"Stop saying old hag!"
Aunt Tracey shouts.

"Tia, Mommy just said old hag."
Trish and Tia laugh.

"Okay, girls," Aunt Tracey asks,
"who wrote this sentence
and left it here?
Please don't do it again.
I don't need my children
calling people names."

I side-glance to Mom.
Her face is redder
than the shirt she's wearing.

"Oh crud," I whisper.

MAJOR FREAK-OUT

Mom waits for
Aunt Tracey to leave
before she freaks out.

"Claire, I warned you!
No Qualifiers."

"But I—"

"NO!"

My brain is buzzing
and I'm dizzy.

I feel like

I

   can't

    breathe.

"Mom, don't.
Don't take gymnastics away from her," Bethany says.
"It's not fair.
She's really, really good at it."

"Yes, she's good
but I'm not putting up with
her games anymore.
She needs to be focusing on

schoolwork

not writing notes that call teachers names."

"But, Mom,
you aren't listening.
I've been working
really hard.
Bethany wrote that
to help me with my reading.

I
NEED
HELP."

"Claire, you've taken this
way too far.
You are perfectly capable
of reading on your own.
You've been doing it
since you were little.
I don't know why
you're lying now."

I'm shaking so much
I feel like throwing up.
"It's not a lie, Mom," I say.
"I couldn't read before
and I can't do it now."

"That's it, Claire.
Enough.
You're done."

HIDING

I go to my room
grab the giraffe-print throw
Bethany got me for Christmas
and take it into the closet.

I curl up on the floor
and hide there.

I don't even come down
when Mom calls me for dinner.

When I finally stand up
my legs
are tingling

and I'm stiff
        achy
        and really hungry.

SISTER SUPPORT

I find Bethany in the kitchen,
eating popcorn.

She hugs me
then offers me some.
"We'll figure out something
to make Mom
understand
you aren't fooling around."

"I don't know why
she thinks I'm lying.
Why would anyone make that up?"

"Attention, maybe?

Really, I think she has
a hard time accepting things
that she thinks might be bad
for us."

"Is a learning disability bad?"
I swallow the worry
building in my throat
but it sticks there
like the flaky part
of a popcorn kernel.

"No. But some people
think it is
because they think
people with learning disabilities
aren't smart."

SMART PEOPLE

"Albert Einstein was a scientist," I tell Bethany.
"He did a lot of great things.
Right?"

"Yes," she says.
"He was super smart."

"He had a learning disability.
Mr. McKay told me.
His learning disability
didn't limit him.
I bet there are more people
like that."

Bethany is already on her phone,
searching.
"There are a lot of them.

What's your plan?"

THE PLAN

"Well, if there are a lot of people with
learning disabilities
who have done amazing things
and we put their photos
and what they did on sticky notes
and post them all over the house
like you did with my sentences

Mom will find them.
Maybe she'll see
that me having a disability
won't hold me back."

MAKING THE LIST

Bethany is a Google queen.
"Tom Cruise," she says.

"The actor guy?"

"I guess. And Henry Winkler.
He co-writes those Hank books, right?"
She looks up from the screen.

"I don't read books, remember?
Besides he was an actor and director first."

"Jamie Oliver," she says.

"The Naked Chef?"

"Really? He cooks naked?" she asks.

"No . . . at least I don't think so.
I think it's just his nickname."

"Since when do you cook?"

"Mom watched his show once."

"ONCE? And you remember?" she says.
"Oh, and Thomas Edison."

"Let there be light . . . bulbs."
I laugh at my own joke.
"He didn't invent them though.
He just figured out how to make them
stay lit longer."

Bethany stops Googling
and blinks at me for long enough
that I know she's thinking

I'm weird.

But then she says,
"Claire, for someone
with a learning disability
you're really smart."

Hearing those words
from Bethany
makes me feel like I would
if I had just landed

a Biles vault.

EXECUTION

Pasting pictures
and calligraphy names,
Bethany and I decorate
sticky notes.

Each one saying
what great things
the person did.

"Hang these up all at once?"
Bethany asks.
"Or spread them out
over the week?"

"Spread them out.
All at once will mean
a sticky mess.
Mom will get mad."

"Okay," Bethany says.
"It's time for you to tell Dad."

I gulp
and nod.

Bethany is right again.

MONDAY PHONE CALL WITH DAD

"Dad, I need your full attention," I say.
"This is important."

"Give me a second."
Dad carries his computer
into the other room
and closes the door.

I should have told him
I needed his full attention
before.

"What's up?" he asks.

"I can't read
and Mom won't believe me.
She won't let me take
the tests to see
what's wrong with me."

"Nothing's wrong with you," Dad says.

He doesn't believe me either.
I sink lower in my chair
and try to swallow the lump
growing in my throat.

"Nothing's wrong with you,"
he repeats, "but you may learn
a different way than other people."

The lump doesn't go down—
instead it gets caught
and boomerangs
up to my eyes.

I take a deep breath
and let it out slowly.

He believes me.

Dad touches the screen
like he's trying
to wipe away my tears.

"Mom won't believe me
and I want you both
to sign some papers
to let me get tested
for a learning disability."

"I'll try to help
convince your mom."

"Thanks." I sniff.

"It might not be easy.
I'm not her favorite person
but your mom really loves you."

"I know."

NO FLIPPING WAY!

Mrs. Rose stands behind me again,
watching me write.

She sighs
and snatches my paper away
so fast I accidentally write
on the desk.

She puts her hand on my shoulder
when I automatically
start to stand to go to the office.

"My fault."
She leans in close to me
and takes her big yellow highlighter
and draws a line down the side of my page.
"When you start a new line
bring your letters all the way
to this line," she whispers.
"Your letters are getting
much better.
It's time you worked
on where you put them."

I never expected
Mrs. Rose
to be on my side
before Mom.

CONFRONTATION

"Claire, Bethany!" Mom calls.
"Get down here
right now."

"What did you do?" I ask
as we step out of our rooms.

Bethany rolls her eyes.
"I think it's about what
we've been doing.
You know.
The Post-its."

"Oh yeah . . .
that."

Mom is holding up
our Post-it
of Isaac Newton.

"I'm overworked and tired
and have enough to deal with
without this nonsense.
Will you two
just stop?"

Her words hit me
so fast

I don't know
how to feel.

My emotions
are like a whole team of gymnasts
tumbling toward each other
at the same time.

"IT'S NOT NONSENSE!" I shout.
"IT IS ABSOLUTELY NOT
NONSENSE.
The only nonsense
is you not believing me!"

"Go to your room.
You're grounded."

"NO, MOM.
You have to listen.

You've already taken away
the most important thing

and I'm still saying it.

    I
      CANNOT
                    READ."

"Claire, enough."

"Do you know what happens
when I try to read?
DO YOU KNOW, Mom?

I get dizzy
and headaches
and want to throw up.

You're the only one
who doesn't believe me.
Why won't you believe me?"

I don't bother to wait
for her answer
before I stomp to my room.

ACCEPTANCE

"Claire." Mom
knocks at my bedroom door.
"Can I come in?"

"Are you going to yell at me?"
I ask.

"No."

"Then yes. Come in."

Mom opens the door
and takes a deep breath
like she's about to perform
a floor routine
in front of a crowd.
"You're not joking, are you?
You really
can't read."

"Not really.
Not like I'm supposed to."

A tear rolls down Mom's cheek.

"It's not your fault,
really. Mr. McKay
and Mrs. French say
I just see things different."

Mom sits beside me on the bed.
"I should have noticed before.
I should have accepted it before.
What kind of mother refuses to
get help
for her child?"

"I hid it well.
Even Mr. McKay says so.
No one knew
I couldn't read, Mom.
Not you.
Not Mrs. Rose.
No one but me."

"I'm sorry," Mom says.

I CAN FLY

I step up
to the bars
during practice.

Breathe.

SWING
    SWING
        SWING

GIANT
    PIROUETTE
        FULL TWIST

FULL
    AWAY.

Again.

SWING
    SWING
        SWING

GIANT
    PIROUETTE
        FULL TWIST

FULL
    AWAY.

State Qualifiers
here I come.

SILENT READING

When Mrs. Rose
tells us,
"Take out your silent reading books,"
I stand up.

"Claire, where are you going?"

"I'm going to see Mrs. French."
"SPED," Tony coughs.

I lean over my desk
and whisper,
"I can get help with my reading
but you'll always be a jerk."

SMACKDOWN

While I'm cooling down
after jogging
with Bethany and Emma Lea
I see a caterpillar
inching its way along
the low branch of a tree
outside our house.

I raise my hand
to smack it down

but instead I stop and
watch and the caterpillar
plummets
to the ground
determining its own future.

I kneel
to get a closer look
as it creeps along the grass
working hard to grow
by munching away
like it's saying to me

Who are you to say
I will never be?

I look up at Emma Lea
watching me.

"I thought you were going to smack it."

"No," I say. "No reason to."

FULL TWIST FULL AWAY

I've never been afraid
of working hard
to nail a skill.

I am going to have to
put in the work
one step
at a time
before my reading
flows
as smoothly as my

GIANT
PIROUETTE
FULL TWIST
FULL
AWAY

at State Qualifiers.

I've never been afraid
of working hard
to nail a skill.

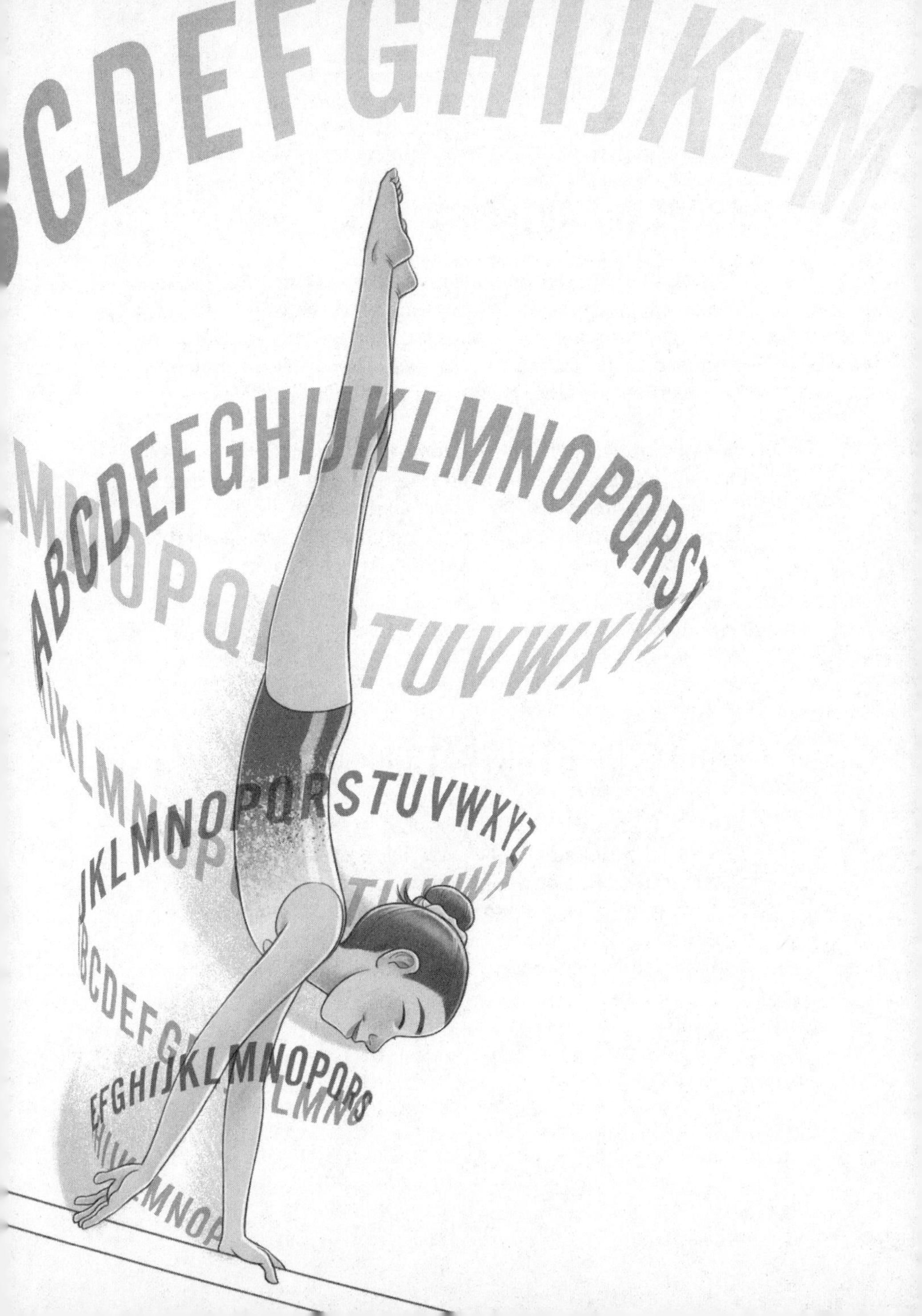

ABOUT THE AUTHOR

Alma Fullerton was born in Ottawa, Ontario, Canada, and lived in Ontario, British Columbia, Nova Scotia, and Germany with her large military family. Growing up, she struggled with reading. At the age of nine, with the help of her fourth-grade teacher, she realized she had dyslexia.

By ninth grade, Alma loved reading and wanted to be a writer, but was always told she could never write a book because of her learning disability. Today Alma speaks to children about overcoming obstacles and not giving up when it comes to their goals and dreams. She is the author of twelve books.

ABOUT THE ILLUSTRATOR

Sarah Mensinga has illustrated several books, including *Different: A Great Thing to Be!*, *Everyone Belongs*, and the Trillium Sisters series. She's also contributed comics to anthologies such as *Flight* and *Fablewood*, worked on animated films, and written three books. Born in Toronto, Canada, Sarah now lives in Texas with her family. Find more of her work at *SarahMensinga.com*.

ACKNOWLEDGMENTS

Special thanks to my writing group, Anne Marie Pace, Kathryn Erskine, Kristy Dempsey, Linda Urban, Tanya Goulette Seale, Katy Duffield, and Cassandra Reigel Whetstone, who have been there from the start.

Thanks to my agent, Deborah Warren, and editor, Catherine Frank, who believed enough in this book to make it come to life.